Police Officer

Lucy M. George

Ando Twin

PC Seth is a police officer.

He wears a smart uniform, with a belt to carry his equipment, a hat and a badge!

It's PC Seth's job to protect
people in the community.

PC Seth has an early shift today.
He arrives at the police station right on time!

The sergeant is briefing the team for the day.
"Good morning, Sergeant!" calls PC Seth.

"Hello, Seth," says
the sergeant. Then
he gives everyone
a job for the day.

Some officers go
out on horseback
to patrol the streets.

Some go to a
crime scene...

...but PC Seth and
PC Thea are going
to the local festival!

They go to their police car and
check everything is working.

NeeeeeeeNaaaaaaaw!

PC Thea tests the special flashing lights
and the siren that makes a loud noise.

PC Thea drives through the busy
streets on the way to the festival.

PC Seth keeps an eye on the traffic
to make sure everyone is driving safely.

The festival is busy. People are out in the sun eating, playing games and enjoying themselves.

PC Seth and PC Thea patrol the grounds.

They give a family directions...

...help someone whose car is stuck in the mud...

...and ask a stallholder to keep the path clear.

Suddenly PC Seth feels a tug on his arm.

It's a little boy.

"I've lost my mum and dad," the boy cries.
"Oh dear," says PC Seth. "What's your name?"

"Alex," whispers the little boy.
"Don't worry, Alex, we'll find them," says PC Seth.

PC Seth asks Alex where he saw his parents last and what they look like.

Then PC Seth has an idea. "Do you have their phone number?" he asks.

Alex looks in his bag.

"Here!" he says. "Dad wrote it down in case of an emergency."

"Clever Dad!" says PC Seth. He tries calling but there's no signal.

"We'll never find them!" Alex says.
He starts to cry. He wants his mum and dad.

"Don't worry, Alex, let's try the meeting
point," says PC Thea. "We will find them!"

As they get close, Alex
thinks he can see his parents...

MEETING POINT

"He came and asked for our help," explains PC Seth.

"Well done, Alex," says his mum.

PC Seth and PC Thea decide to get an ice cream.

"It's your turn to buy them,"
says PC Thea with a grin.

"Fair enough," says PC Seth, "but I'm driving home!"

What else does PC Seth do?

Directs traffic.

Helps investigate crime scenes.

Teaches children about safety.

Arrests criminals.

What does PC Seth need?

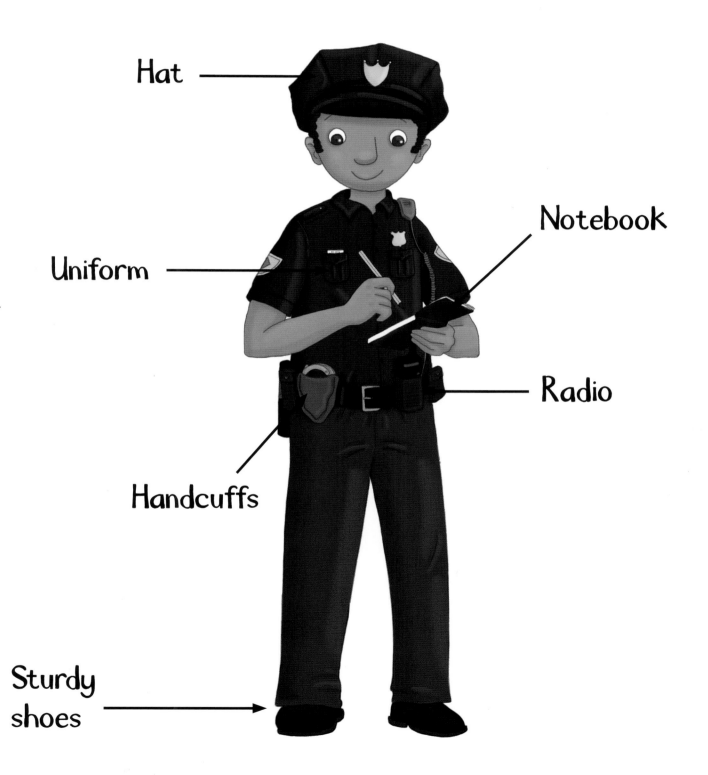

Hat

Uniform

Handcuffs

Notebook

Radio

Sturdy shoes

Other busy people

Here are some of the other busy people police officers work with.

Police sergeants run the police station, managing the police officers and co-ordinating teams on investigations.

Forensic scientists examine evidence from crime scenes, including photographs, fingerprints and samples.

Police dog handlers use highly trained dogs to help them find evidence at a crime scene.

Family liaison officers work with families affected by crime or an accident. An officer suppports the family and tells them what is happening.

Next steps

- Alex got separated from his mum and dad at the festival. Have you ever lost the person looking after you? Were you scared? What did you do?

- Alex found a police officer when he was lost. What did the police officer ask him for? Do you know what to do if you get lost?

- PC Seth was on patrol at the festival. Ask the children why the police were there and what jobs they had to do at the festival.

- The police have wide and varied roles. Discuss these roles with the children and ask them why they are important. Ask them to imagine what would happen if there was no police force.

- Discuss the other jobs in the police force and what the children think about these roles. Would the children like to become police officers one day or work for the police? Which job would the children like to do most?

Inspiring | Educating | Creating | Entertaining

Brimming with creative inspiration, how-to projects, and useful information to enrich your everyday life, quarto.com is a favorite destination for those pursuing their interests and passions.

Publisher: Maxime Boucknooghe
Editorial Director: Victoria Garrard
Art Director: Miranda Snow
Editor: Sophie Hallam
Designer: Victoria Kimonidou
Consultant: PC Yvonne Monaghan

Copyright © QED Publishing 2016

First published in the UK in 2016 by
QED Publishing
Part of The Quarto Group
The Old Brewery
6 Blundell Street
London, N7 9BH

A catalogue record for this book is available from the British Library.

ISBN 978 1 78493 835 2

Manufactured in Guangdong, China TT042022

**For Granny Wilson
- AndoTwin**

**For Mitchell & Rhys
- Lucy M. George**